God Gave Us Fathers and Mothers

Written by Rebecca Newswanger

Illustrated by Maria Steiner

Copyright 2009
Rod and Staff Publishers, Inc.

Rod and Staff Books
(Milestone Ministries)
800-761-0234 or 541-466-3231
www.RodandStaffBooks.com

Catalog no. 2785

1 2 3 4 5 — 18 17 16 15 14 13 12 11 10 09

OUR
FATHERS

God gave us fathers, wise and strong;
Wise fathers teach us right from wrong.
Strong fathers work to bring us food;
They help us to be kind and good.

Our fathers read
    God's Word each day;
We learn from them
    To sing and pray.

This father plows
  And plants his field;
He knows God sends
  The fruitful yield.

Here come the cows!
It's time to chore;
This farmer milks
At half-past four.

Bang! Bang! This father
    Works with wood
To build a house
    That's firm and good.

A carpenter
　　Makes wooden chairs,
And tables too,
　　And rails for stairs.

This father teaches
Christian school;
His eager students
Learn each rule.

This father can
Repair a truck;
He'll even tow it
If it's stuck!

A writer,

Plumber,

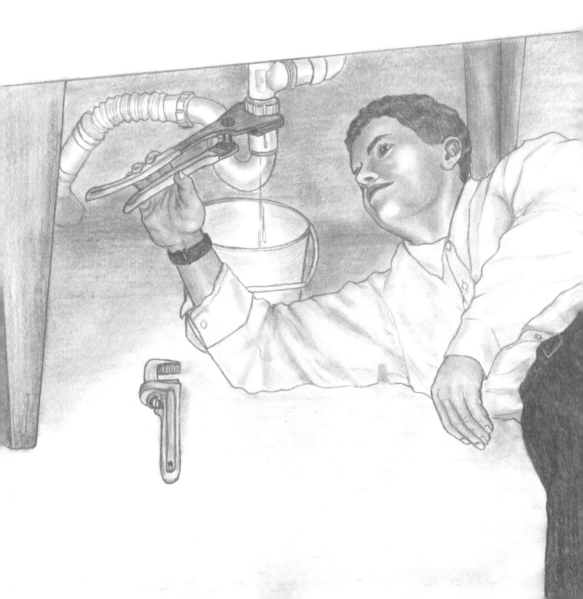

Fisherman—
Let's help our fathers
All we can.

OUR
MOTHERS

God gave us sweet mothers to love us each day;
They teach us to work; they join in our play.
They read us our stories and help us to sing,
And teach us of God, who made everything.

Chop! Chop! Here's a mother
   Who's swinging her hoe;
She works in her garden
   Where vegetables grow.

See, here is a mother
Preparing a stew;
She'll serve bread and salad
And apple pie too.

This mother is making
    Her family's clothes;
She snips, and she irons,
    And carefully sews.

Can you hear the hum
    Of this washing machine?
This mother is keeping
    Her children's clothes clean.

Sh-sh! Mother is rocking
    Her sweet baby dear;
She feeds him and pats him
    And cuddles him near.

Our kind mothers tend us
Whenever we're ill;
They wash dirty dishes
And wipe up each spill.

All day they are working
  For you and for me.
Now don't you suppose
  We should help cheerfully?

We love our dear parents,
And they love the Lord!
They teach us to trust
And obey God's own Word.

When we are obedient
    And walk in God's way,
God blesses our home
    And we're happy each day.